Spy Hunt

By Maria S. Barbo
Illustrated by Duendes del Sur

ISBN 0-439-67840-4

Copyright © 2004 by Hanna-Barbera.
SCOOBY-DOO and all related characters and elements are trademarks of and © Hanna-Barbera.
CARTOON NETWORK and logo are trademarks of and © Cartoon Network.
(s04)
All rights reserved. Published by Scholastic Inc.
SCHOLASTIC, HELLO READER, and associated logos are trademarks and/or registered trademarks of Scholastic Inc.

12 11 10 9 8 7 6 5 4 3 2 1   4 5 6 7 8 9/0

Designed by Louise Bova
Printed in the U.S.A.
First printing, November 2004

SCHOLASTIC INC.
New York   Toronto   London   Auckland   Sydney
Mexico City   New Delhi   Hong Kong   Buenos Aires

It was a long weekend.

 and watched too much .

They played with too many .

They read all their .

They ate all their .

Now, is bored.

is bored, too.

Then, has an idea.

"Let's pretend we are spies!"

says .

 puts on a silly .

 puts on a funny 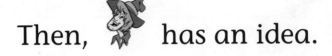 .

"Like, no one will know who we

are, ," says .

 barks.

 likes to play SPY HUNT.

and spy on  .

 uses his super dog to listen.

 hears a noise.

Shwoosh-wooosh — shwoosh.

 sneaks over to the .

But he does not find .

is missing!

There is a mess on her .

Her is open.

Her are gone.

 holds up his .

 takes 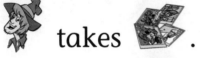 .

"What if a took ?" asks
 .

"Rikes!" barks .

"Zoinks!" cries .

 hides under the .

 hides next to .

But and  must be

brave.

They are super spies.

They will find .

and spy on .

They hide behind the .

 hears a noise.

Drip-drip-drip-drop-drip.

 sees 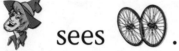 .

 uses his 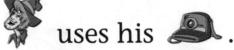 .

Is with ?

Or did a kidnap ?

and  spy on .

 hears a noise.

Tick-tick-tickety-tick.

 sees .

 takes .

Is with ?

Or did a take ?

Is 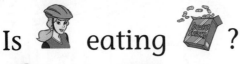 eating 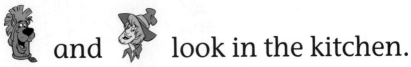 ?

 and look in the kitchen.

A bottle of is gone.

The are missing.

Do drink ?

Do eat ?

Did a hide ?

and are good spies.

But they can't find .

 is not on her .

 is not with .

 is not with .

And is not eating .

Maybe a *really* did take

.

and are sad.

 takes off his .

 takes off his funny .

 puts down his .

 looks at the .

Then, has an idea.

"Zoinks!" says . "A did

not take !"

hears a .

 sees 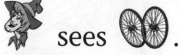 .

A did not take .

 was riding her !

 gives some  .

 barks.

"Scooby-Dooby-Doo!"

Did you spot all the picture clues in this Scooby-Doo mystery?

Each picture clue is on a flash card. Ask a grown-up to cut out the flash cards. Then try reading the words on the back of the cards. The pictures will be your clue.

Reading is fun with Scooby-Doo!